AH CHOO

The Wakefield family was having dinner.

"Ah—" Mr. Wakefield gasped. He closed his eyes and let out a gigantic sneeze. "Ah—ahh—choo!"

"Are you coming down with a cold?" Mrs. Wakefield asked.

Mr. Wakefield rubbed his eyes and shook his head. "No. It feels more like hay fever. It's as though there's a cat in the house."

Jessica suddenly knocked her milk glass over. She stared wide-eyed at Elizabeth. They both knew Mr. Wakefield was sneezing because of Misty.

"What are we going to do?" Jessica whispered in Elizabeth's ear.

"I don't know," Elizabeth whispered back.

Jessica gulped. They had to find a solution, and they had to find it fast!

Bantam Skylark Books in the
SWEET VALLEY KIDS series
Ask your bookseller for the
books you have missed

SWEET VALLEY KIDS

JESSICA'S CAT TRICK

Created by
Francine Pascal

Written by
Molly Mia Stewart

Illustrated by
Ying-Hwa Hu

A BANTAM SKYLARK BOOK®
NEW YORK · TORONTO · LONDON · SYDNEY · AUCKLAND

RL 2, 005–008

JESSICA'S CAT TRICK
A Bantam Skylark Book / March 1990

*Sweet Valley High® and Sweet Valley Kids are
registered trademarks of Francine Pascal*

*Conceived by Francine Pascal
Produced by Daniel Weiss Associates, Inc.
33 West 17th Street
New York, NY 10011*

Cover art by Susan Tang

*Skylark Books is a registered trademark of Bantam Books, a division of
Bantam Doubleday Dell Publishing Group, Inc.*

ISBN 0-553-15768-X

Published simultaneously in the United States and Canada

---

*Bantam Books are published by Bantam Books, a division of Bantam Double-
day Dell Publishing Group, Inc. Its trademark, consisting of the words
"Bantam Books" and the portrayal of a rooster, is Registered in U.S. Patent
and Trademark Office and in other countries. Marca Registrada. Bantam
Books, 666 Fifth Avenue, New York, New York 10103.*

PRINTED IN THE UNITED STATES OF AMERICA

OPM   0 9 8 7 6 5 4 3 2

To Jordan David Adler

CHAPTER 1

The Twins' Secret

"Come on, Jessica," Elizabeth Wakefield said as she jumped off the school bus and grabbed her twin sister's hand. "Let's run home fast."

"OK," Jessica answered.

The girls had a special reason for being in a hurry. A few days earlier, Elizabeth and Jessica had found a cat hiding under some bushes in their backyard. The twins wanted to keep her, but they knew their father and their brother, Steven, were both allergic to cats.

They hoped she hadn't run away.

"Act like everything's normal," Jessica said as she and Elizabeth reached their front door.

Elizabeth nodded. "I will, Jess. I know t' has to stay a secret."

At exactly the same time, both girls crossed their hearts and snapped their fingers twice. It was their own special promise sign, and they always did it together.

Jessica and Elizabeth did almost everything together. They were identical twins, and that meant they were very special best friends. There were times when Elizabeth knew just what Jessica was thinking or what she was about to say. Jessica often knew what Elizabeth was thinking about, too. They shared a bedroom, they wore the same

2

outfits, and they always divided cookies and candy right down the middle.

Jessica and Elizabeth also looked exactly alike. They both had long blond hair with bangs and blue-green eyes. And when they dressed in their matching outfits, most of the kids in their second-grade class couldn't tell them apart. Only by looking at their name bracelets could anyone be sure who was who.

But just because they looked and sounded the same on the *outside,* didn't mean they were the same on the *inside.* Elizabeth liked to make up adventure stories and act them out in the backyard. Jessica preferred to play inside with their dollhouse so she wouldn't get messy. Elizabeth liked school and always did her homework right away. Jessica made faces when she had to open her schoolbooks.

3

She thought school was for whispering with friends instead of learning addition and spelling.

But those differences didn't matter. They would always be best friends.

"Shh!" Elizabeth said, putting one finger on her lips as she opened the door. Jessica tiptoed in behind her.

"Hi, girls!" Mrs. Wakefield greeted them in the front hall.

Elizabeth and Jessica both jumped. "Hi, Mom," Elizabeth said. She looked at her sister and gulped.

"Hi, Mom," Jessica repeated. "We're going to play in the backyard."

Their mother looked surprised. "No snack today?"

"No, thanks," they said at the same time.

"OK. I'll be upstairs if you change your minds."

Once their mother was gone, Elizabeth and Jessica ran out to the backyard. Elizabeth knelt down in front of a bush. "Is she still there?" Jessica asked.

Elizabeth moved a branch away. "Meow!" came a sad cry.

"She sure is!" Elizabeth answered as she pushed her head in until she could see the cat.

"Meow!" the cat cried again. Her long fur was gray and white, and she had white boots on her two front paws. But she also looked dirty and hungry, and she had a bad scratch on one ear.

Jessica crawled in next to Elizabeth. "Oh! She looks so lonely!" Jessica said. She

cuddled the cat gently in her arms until it began to purr.

Elizabeth felt sad as she looked at the cat. "I wish we could keep her," she said.

"I think we should," Jessica decided. "She's been here for three days. That means she doesn't have a home. And she likes us, too."

Elizabeth looked at her sister and at the cat. They knew they couldn't have a cat. But this one *needed* them!

"We could bring her some food out here," Elizabeth said.

Jessica nodded. "We could—"

Just then, there was a tapping sound on the branches over them. Elizabeth's stomach flip-flopped. "It's starting to rain!" she exclaimed.

Jessica gasped. "Now we *have* to take her inside!"

CHAPTER 2

A Cat Named Misty

"You hold her," Jessica said. She carefully put the cat in her sister's arms. "I'll go see if the coast is clear."

Jessica ran through the rain back into the house. "Mom?" she called out.

"I'm in the living room!" her mother answered. "Do you want me for something?"

"No!" Jessica crossed her fingers and hoped her mother would stay where she was. "It's nothing!" On tiptoe, she ran to the back door again, and waved to Elizabeth. "Shhh!" she said as Elizabeth hurried over with the cat in her arms. She looked at her sister and pretended to zip her mouth with a zipper.

As quietly as mice, Jessica and Elizabeth peeked into the kitchen. Then they ran to the door and peeked into the hall.

"All clear," Jessica whispered. Together, they ran through the hall and up the stairs. Once they were in their room, Jessica closed the door and leaned against it. "Phew!" she gasped.

"That was close," Elizabeth said. She put the cat down gently on her bed, and then looked at Jessica. "This is going to be difficult," she added.

Jessica knelt down by the bed and stroked the cat's head. "I know," she agreed. "But she needs us."

Elizabeth knelt next to her, and they both

looked into the cat's eyes. "Let's think of a name," Jessica said.

"I know a pretty one. How about Misty? Because her fur is mostly gray?"

Jessica smiled. "Good idea! How are you, Misty?" she asked the cat. Misty purred, and slowly blinked her yellow eyes. "She likes that name!" Jessica decided.

"Maybe we should fix her a bed in the closet," Elizabeth suggested. "That way, no one will see her."

"Good idea," Jessica said. The twins shared a large walk-in closet. "I'll get her some milk while you do that."

Elizabeth looked worried. "Don't let Mom see what you're doing."

"I won't," Jessica said. "I know a good plan."

All the way down the stairs, Jessica's heart beat faster. She thought of all kinds of reasons for wanting some milk. She was about to tell her mother she needed milk for a science experiment when she thought of the best reason.

"Mom?" she said, going into the living room.

Mrs. Wakefield was looking through big books of wallpaper designs. She was taking a course on interior decorating, and had to do a lot of studying. "What is it, honey?" she asked.

"Can I have a glass of milk? I'm thirsty." Jessica opened her eyes very wide.

Her mother smiled. "Of course. You know you don't have to ask."

"OK," Jessica said, feeling relieved. She ran into the kitchen and poured milk into a glass. Then she realized Misty wouldn't be able to drink from a tall glass, so Jessica poured the milk into a bowl. Watching to make sure her mother didn't see her, Jessica climbed upstairs carefully. She had to walk very slowly to keep from spilling any milk over the side of the bowl.

"I made it," Jessica whispered when she got back to the room.

Elizabeth was kneeling by the closet. "Good. She's in here."

"Here you go, Misty," Jessica said. She set the bowl down by the cat, and Misty began lapping up the milk. She seemed very thirsty.

"Misty really likes that," Elizabeth said. She smiled at Jessica. "She must be glad we found her."

"So am I!" Jessica said. Elizabeth had

made a cozy bed out of a soft blanket. "Do you think she wants something else besides milk?"

Elizabeth shrugged. "I don't know," she said slowly.

Jessica's eyes lit up. "I know! Some tuna fish! Cats like fish."

"Good idea!" Elizabeth said, jumping up. "I'll go down this time."

Mrs. Wakefield was still in the living room as Elizabeth tiptoed into the kitchen. She found a can of tuna fish, and took the can opener out of a drawer. Then she heard footsteps!

Elizabeth quickly popped the can and the can opener under her shirt, and folded her arms across it. There was a big lump around her waist.

"You girls are very quiet today. Is anything wrong?" Mrs. Wakefield asked, coming into the kitchen.

Elizabeth shook her head several times. "No, Mom. Everything's fine. I'm going upstairs now," she said as she backed up to the door. Her arms were still folded tightly across her waist.

Mrs. Wakefield looked puzzled. "Do you feel well, Elizabeth?"

"Yes!" Elizabeth shouted. Then she turned and ran. It was going to be harder than she thought to keep Misty a secret!

CHAPTER 3

The Secret Is Out

Before school started the next day, Elizabeth and Jessica told their friends about bringing Misty up to their room.

"It's a secret, you guys," Elizabeth said to Amy Sutton, Eva Simpson, Ellen Riteman, and Lila Fowler. All the girls had found Misty together over the weekend.

Amy nodded. "I won't tell anyone," she promised.

"It's good that she stayed in your backyard," Eva added. "She could have starved. I had a kitty when I lived in Jamaica, but it ran away when I was five."

Eva had just moved to Sweet Valley, but she was already a good friend. She had a pretty, singsong way of talking because she had grown up in Jamaica, one of the islands of the West Indies.

"If I could have a cat, I'd name it after my favorite person on TV," Ellen told them. "Tippy Tiger."

"Tippy Tiger is a cartoon, not a person," Lila said in a know-it-all voice.

Ellen's face turned pink. "I'd still name it Tippy if I had one," she muttered.

"Hi, everyone," Caroline Pearce said as she pushed her way into their group. "What are you talking about?"

No one said anything at first. Elizabeth looked at her sister nervously. Caroline talked a lot. She would *never* keep their secret. And she only lived two houses away from them. If Caroline knew about Misty, she would blab it to everyone!

"They're hiding a cat in their bedroom closet," Lila announced.

"Lila!" Jessica's mouth opened wide. Lila was Jessica's best friend after Elizabeth, but Elizabeth didn't like her very much. Lila was very bossy.

Caroline's eyes widened. "I bet you'll get in trouble," she said. "I bet you'll have to give it away."

"We will not!" Jessica said angrily. "You're just saying that to be mean!"

Elizabeth looked at Amy, but didn't say anything. She was worried about hiding Misty in their room. She knew it wasn't right. But what else could they do? Misty would have

19

starved if they hadn't taken her in. Or, she might have gotten sick out in the rain.

"Don't tell anyone else," Eva suggested. "We must all keep it a secret."

"Keep what a secret?" Winston Egbert asked. No one had heard him come up. He was the skinniest boy in their class.

"None of your beeswax," Jessica grumbled, crossing her arms in front of her.

But Caroline pointed at Elizabeth and Jessica and said, "They found a cat and they aren't allowed to have one. I bet they're going to get into a lot of trouble for keeping it in their closet."

"Gee." Winston looked disappointed. "I wish I could have a cat."

"I have two cats," a voice said shyly. Everyone looked around. It was Lois Waller. "Their names are Snowball and Peekaboo."

"We shouldn't have told even one person," Elizabeth whispered in her sister's ear. "Now almost everybody knows!"

Jessica shrugged. It was too late now.

"Can I come over after school and see Misty?" Amy asked Elizabeth.

"Well . . ." Elizabeth began. Amy was her best friend after Jessica, so she couldn't say no. She just hoped their mother didn't find out their secret. "OK," she agreed in a low voice.

"What about me?" Lila interrupted. "Can't I come, too?"

Jessica frowned. "OK, but no one else."

Elizabeth and Jessica looked at each other. Now that so many people knew about Misty, how could they keep their family from finding out?

CHAPTER 4

A Special Playdate

After school, Amy and Lila came home on the bus with the twins.

"Come on, you guys," Jessica whispered as they entered the house and quickly went upstairs.

Elizabeth closed the door tightly when they reached the bedroom. "Misty stays in here while we're at school," she told them, opening the closet.

"Meow!" Misty rubbed against each twin's ankles. She looked glad to see them.

"Ohhh!" Amy said. She knelt down and

stroked Misty under the chin. Misty stretched and arched her back happily. "She's so pretty!"

"She is," Lila agreed. "But why is her stomach sagging like that?"

Jessica frowned. Misty did have a very large stomach, but she didn't know why. "Maybe her stomach's big because we gave her so much tuna fish when we found her," she suggested.

The others looked unsure.

"I think she's OK now," Elizabeth said. "But she likes to sleep in here all day. She's always sleepy." Then she reached into the back of the closet, and pulled out a shoe box filled with dirt from the backyard.

"This is her bathroom," she whispered.

Lila giggled.

"It smells a little," Jessica said, pinching her nose shut.

Amy nudged Elizabeth. "We could empty it out," she said.

Jessica hoped they would. She certainly didn't want to. "We'll stay with Misty while you go," she said.

Elizabeth put the lid back on the shoe box, and then tucked it under her arm. "OK. Let's go," she said to Amy. The two girls hurried out the door. Before Jessica realized what was happening, Misty ran out, too.

"Oh, no!" she gasped. "Get her!"

Jessica and Lila ran out into the hallway. "Heeeere, Misty," Jessica whispered. Her heart was beating hard. What if Misty ran downstairs?

"There she is," Lila said in a low voice.

Misty was sitting at the top of the stairs, looking down. Jessica scooped her up, and took her back into the bedroom. Lila shut the door.

"That was close," Lila said.

"It sure was," Jessica agreed, hugging Misty. "Don't be naughty anymore," she told the cat. Misty purred and rubbed her cheek on Jessica's arm.

Lila's eyes widened suddenly. "Someone's coming!"

Jessica quickly put Misty into the closet. Footsteps passed by the doorway. Then they stopped.

"Ah—ah—ah—CHOO!" Steven sneezed loud enough for Jessica and Lila to hear. They stared at each other. They heard his footsteps going to his room.

"How long can you keep Misty a secret?" Lila asked.

Jessica gulped. "I don't know."

"You can't keep her in here forever!" Lila went on. "What are you going to do?"

Jessica gulped again. She didn't know what to say.

After Lila and Amy went home, the twins sat at the kitchen table doing homework. Steven was working on a model car.

"Can Eva come over tomorrow, Mom?" Elizabeth asked as Mrs. Wakefield came in to start dinner.

"And Ellen?" Jessica chimed in. Their other friends wanted to meet Misty, too.

Mrs. Wakefield looked surprised. "But you had friends over to play today."

Jessica and Elizabeth looked at each other. "We know," Jessica said. "But we want some *other* friends to come over."

"We'll see," their mother said.

Steven pretended to choke himself. "Today was like an invasion of girls," he muttered. "Don't let any more come over."

Jessica stuck her tongue out at her brother.

"That's funny," Mrs. Wakefield said, looking in a cupboard. "I thought I had two cans of tuna fish in here. I was going to make tuna salad but I see I don't have enough."

Jessica lowered her eyes, and glanced at her sister. Elizabeth's face was bright pink. Jessica tried to think of a good explanation.

"Maybe Steven ate it," Jessica suggested.

"I did not!" Steven said. "Maybe there's an alien invader living in the house who's eating our food. There's hardly any milk left, either."

Jessica's stomach flip-flopped, and Elizabeth dropped her pencil. Steven didn't know how close to the truth he was!

CHAPTER 5

Close Call!

Elizabeth and Jessica were finishing their cereal the next morning when the front doorbell rang.

"Who could that be?" Mr. Wakefield asked. He put down his newspaper and headed out of the room. They all heard him sneeze in the hallway. In a few moments, he came back.

"Look who's here," he said.

Elizabeth and Jessica both turned around to look. It was Caroline Pearce! Elizabeth was too surprised to say hello.

"Hi," Caroline said. She was holding her

books and her lunch box in her arms. "Can I walk to the bus stop with you?"

Elizabeth nodded. "Sure," she said. Jessica kicked her under the table.

"Would you like some orange juice, Caroline?" Mrs. Wakefield asked.

"No, thank you." Caroline came and sat down next to Elizabeth. She leaned close enough to whisper. "Can I see the you-know-what?" she asked right in Elizabeth's ear.

Elizabeth's eyes widened. She stared at her parents, but they had not heard Caroline's question. She looked at Jessica. If she said no, maybe Caroline would tattle on them!

"OK," she agreed slowly. She didn't know what else to do. "Mom, can we be excused?"

Mrs. Wakefield nodded. "Yes. Go get ready for school."

The twins and Caroline hurried out of the

kitchen. "She wants to see Misty," Elizabeth whispered to Jessica.

"Caroline!" Jessica looked angry. "You're going to spoil everything."

Caroline shook her head. "No, I won't. I promise! Can I see her?"

"Come on," Elizabeth said. They ran up the stairs and into their bedroom. "Here she is," Elizabeth said, opening the closet.

Caroline's eyes lit up. "Oh, she's so nice!" She sat down next to Misty and tickled her chin. "You're so lucky!"

Elizabeth and Jessica looked at each other. Elizabeth was surprised at how much Caroline liked Misty. Maybe she wouldn't tell their secret, after all.

"Hurry up, girls!" came Mrs. Wakefield's voice. She was just outside the door to the twins' room.

"Quick!" Jessica gasped. "Put Misty in the closet and shut the door!"

The moment Misty was back in the closet, Mrs. Wakefield walked into the bedroom. "It's time to get the bus," she reminded them.

Elizabeth nodded. "OK, Mom."

Their mother turned to go out, but then she stopped and sniffed the air. "What is that? It smells like fish in here."

Elizabeth's cheeks got hot and then cold. From where she was standing, she could see the empty tuna fish can in the trash basket by her desk. What was she going to say? "Ummm . . ."

"I have a tuna sandwich for lunch," Caroline said suddenly. She held up her lunch box. "I think it's leaking."

Elizabeth stared at Caroline. What a smart answer!

"That must be it," Mrs. Wakefield said with a chuckle.

"Meow!"

Everyone froze. Mrs. Wakefield looked puzzled. "What on earth . . . ?"

"Ow!" Caroline said. She put one hand on her mouth. "It's my loose tooth! I didn't mean to make such a loud noise," she apologized.

Mrs. Wakefield smiled. "That's all right. Now hurry up, girls, or you'll miss the bus." She left the room.

For a few seconds, no one spoke. Then Elizabeth let her breath out. "Thanks, Caroline!" she said. "You were great!"

"You sure were," Jessica said. She looked surprised. "Thanks for not telling on us."

"I wouldn't tell on you," Caroline said. "I just wanted to see the kitty."

Elizabeth looked at her sister. She could tell they were both thinking the same thing. Maybe Caroline wasn't such a tattletale after all.

CHAPTER 6

Ah Choo!

Jessica and Elizabeth were watching television in the living room when their mother came in.

"Whose turn is it to set the table?" Mrs. Wakefield asked.

It was Jessica's turn, but she pretended not to hear. Setting the table was her least favorite chore.

"I'll do it," Elizabeth said, standing up.

Their mother raised her eyebrows. "That means it must be Jessica's turn. Come on, young lady."

"OK," Jessica said with a sigh. She stood up and walked slowly to the door.

"I'll help you," Elizabeth offered.

The table was set just in time for dinner. Mr. Wakefield carried a platter of roast chicken into the dining room, but before he put it down, he stopped.

"Ah—" he gasped. He closed his eyes and made a funny face. "Ah—ahh—"

"Let me take that," Mrs. Wakefield said, taking the platter out of his hands.

"CHOO!" Mr. Wakefield let out a gigantic sneeze.

Jessica sneaked a quick look at her sister. Elizabeth was sitting in her seat, carefully unfolding her napkin. Jessica concentrated on pouring herself a glass of milk.

"Are you coming down with a cold?" Mrs. Wakefield asked.

Mr. Wakefield rubbed his eyes and shook his head. "No. It feels more like hay fever, but it's a little too early in the season for that."

"I've got hay fever, too," Steven chimed in. "My throat feels all scratchy." He made a groaning, choking sound in his throat to show what he meant.

"Hmm. I wonder what it could be," Mrs. Wakefield said thoughtfully.

Jessica didn't dare look at Elizabeth again. *They* knew what it could be. It was Misty.

As their father started serving dinner, he said, "You know, it's as though there's a cat in the house."

Jessica suddenly knocked her milk glass over.

"Jessica!" Mrs. Wakefield jumped up and began to mop up the spill with her napkin.

"Sorry," Jessica said. She stared wide-eyed at Elizabeth.

Elizabeth didn't say anything. She just helped clean up the puddle of milk.

"What are we going to do?" Jessica whispered in Elizabeth's ear while the others were busy helping.

"I don't know," Elizabeth whispered back.

Jessica gulped. They had to find a solution, and they had to find it fast!

CHAPTER 7

A Home for Misty

"We have to do something about Misty," Elizabeth told Jessica as they walked to the bus stop in the morning.

Jessica looked behind them to see if anyone could hear. "But I don't know what to do," she said, turning around again.

"I think we have to give her away," Elizabeth said in a sad voice.

"No!" Jessica shouted. Her blue eyes got round. "I want to keep her!"

Elizabeth nodded sadly. "I do, too, but we

can't. We're being sneaky and Misty is making Daddy and Steven sick."

Jessica stopped on the sidewalk. They had almost reached the bus stop, where Todd Wilkins, Caroline Pearce, and Charlie Cashman were waiting with a group of other kids.

"I think we have to," Elizabeth went on. "But maybe we could give her to someone who lives near us."

"Then we could visit her!" Jessica said, sounding more hopeful.

Elizabeth nodded. "That's right."

At the same time, they both looked at Caroline. Charlie Cashman had taken her lunch box, and was looking inside it.

"You give that back, Charlie!" Caroline yelled. She tried to grab it, but Charlie

raised the lunch box above his head. "I'm telling on you!" Caroline shouted.

"I'm telling on you!" Charlie repeated. He tossed the lunch box back to her. "This is a gross lunch, anyway."

Caroline sounded angry as she checked her sandwich. "If you ruined it, I'm telling Mrs. Becker."

Elizabeth and Jessica looked at each other. Caroline wasn't their favorite person, but she seemed to like Misty a lot. And she lived so close by.

"Should we ask her?" Elizabeth said. She knew her twin sister would know who she was talking about.

Jessica poked Elizabeth with her elbow. "Yes, but you ask her."

"OK, let's go," Elizabeth said.

Together they walked up to Caroline.

"We have to talk to you," Elizabeth said.

Jessica nodded. "It's a secret meeting. Come on."

The twins walked to the big oak tree on the corner, and Caroline followed them.

"What is it?" she asked, sounding both curious and excited.

Elizabeth lowered her voice. "First you have to promise not to tell anyone what we ask you," she said.

Caroline looked at Elizabeth, then at Jessica, and back at Elizabeth. "OK," she whispered.

"Promise," Jessica said.

"I promise." Caroline crossed her heart and nodded seriously. "I won't tell."

"OK," Elizabeth said. "We want to know if you want to keep Misty."

Caroline gasped. "For real?"

"For real," Jessica said. She frowned. "But you can only have her if you promise to take *good* care of her."

"I will," Caroline said, nodding fast. "I really will."

Elizabeth felt relieved. "Do you think you can have her?"

Caroline's expression became serious. "I have to ask my parents first," she said. "I don't do anything without their permission."

That made Elizabeth feel terrible. She and Jessica were keeping Misty without their parents' permission and Elizabeth knew it was wrong.

"Do you think they'll say yes?" Jessica wanted to know.

Caroline shrugged her shoulders. "I don't know. I sure hope so."

Elizabeth and Jessica looked at each other. They hoped so, too. If Caroline couldn't take Misty, who would?

CHAPTER 8

What's Wrong
with Misty?

"Hi, girls," Mrs. Wakefield said when the twins walked into the kitchen after school. She was busy drawing on graph paper. Jessica could see it was a plan of a room with all the chairs and tables and couches in a special arrangement.

"Is that your homework for decorating class, Mom?" Jessica asked. Elizabeth walked to the refrigerator to get Misty's milk.

"That's right," their mother answered. She looked over at Elizabeth. "Do you both want milk again?"

Elizabeth froze, but Jessica nodded quickly. "Yes, please. Can we drink it upstairs?"

"Of course. You two sure are drinking a lot of milk lately," Mrs. Wakefield said.

Jessica opened her eyes wide. "We like milk."

"That's right," Elizabeth agreed. "We love milk."

With their glasses full, the twins hurried upstairs to see Misty. "Let's share this one," Jessica said after she took a sip of her milk.

Elizabeth nodded, and opened the closet door. "Hi, Misty." She poured her glass of milk into Misty's bowl.

"Meow," Misty purred very quietly. She didn't get up from her soft bed.

Jessica knelt down by the cat. "Hi," she said, rubbing Misty's chin. "I wonder why she doesn't get up. She always stands up and stretches when we come home."

"I don't know," Elizabeth said slowly. She frowned. "She isn't drinking her milk, either."

Jessica was worried. "You don't think she's sick, do you?" she asked. "Why isn't she eating?"

Elizabeth shook her head. "I don't know. Maybe she'll try the cat food Lois gave me."

Lois Waller had brought in a small paper bag full of dry cat chow from home so the twins could give Misty real cat food. Elizabeth got it out of her bookbag and placed a few pieces in front of Misty. The cat sniffed at them, but didn't eat any. She meowed again softly.

"Liz!" Jessica said in alarm. "What's wrong with her?"

Instead of answering, Elizabeth just

watched the cat. Misty stood up, turned around on her bed, scratched at the blanket with her claws, and curled up again. She looked up at them and blinked.

"Meow," she cried. Her mouth was open and she began to pant, but she wouldn't drink her milk.

"Liz!" Jessica felt tears come to her eyes and she grabbed Elizabeth's hand. "I think she's sick!"

Elizabeth nodded and held Jessica's hand tightly. "Maybe she'll get better if she rests," she said, trying to sound hopeful.

But Jessica didn't think so. She was sure Misty was telling them she didn't feel well *at all*.

"Let's see if she wants to play," Elizabeth suggested. She found a pink hair ribbon on her dresser, and waved it in front of Misty. "Come on, Misty. Catch it!"

Jessica watched silently. Misty looked up at the dangling ribbon but she didn't even lift a paw.

"What if she—" Jessica didn't finish her question. Her throat felt tight.

Elizabeth took a deep breath. "She might need to go to the animal doctor," she said. Her voice sounded scared. "I think we should tell Mom."

Jessica started to cry. Tears ran down her face as she pulled Misty onto her lap. Misty let out another unhappy meow.

"We're going to get into so much trouble!" Jessica wailed.

"But what else can we do? Misty's sick." Elizabeth asked, sniffling.

Jessica nodded. No matter what, they had to make sure Misty was all right.

CHAPTER 9

Mom to the Rescue

Elizabeth gently took Misty out of Jessica's arms, and put her back on the blanket. "Do you think Mom will know what to do?" Jessica asked.

"Yes," Elizabeth said firmly.

Mrs. Wakefield was still drawing on graph paper in the kitchen. The twins walked over to the table. Elizabeth was worried their mother would be angry with them, and she was afraid to speak. But the thought of Misty alone and sick upstairs made her feel brave. "Mom?" She began.

"What is it, honey?" Mrs. Wakefield asked without looking up. She drew a line with the help of her ruler.

"Mom, we have to tell you something," Elizabeth whispered. Jessica squeezed her hand.

Their mother looked up, frowning. "What's wrong?"

Jessica sniffled, and a tear rolled down her cheek.

"Are you sick?" Mrs. Wakefield asked.

"No, but Misty is," Jessica cried.

Mrs. Wakefield looked puzzled. "Who's Misty?"

"Come on," Elizabeth said. She and Jessica led the way upstairs, and their mother followed. "This is Misty," Elizabeth said, opening their bedroom closet.

Misty got up and stretched out on the floor outside the closet. "Meow."

Mrs. Wakefield stared down at the cat in surprise. She didn't say anything at all, and Elizabeth began to feel even more worried. Maybe their mother was going to be *really* angry.

"We found her in the backyard," Jessica said in a shaky voice. "She was starving and hurt and it was raining! We *had* to bring her inside!"

"We didn't mean to be sneaky, Mom," Elizabeth added. "But Misty needed us. And we're trying to find a good home for her. We know she can't stay with us."

Mrs. Wakefield knelt down, too, and scratched between Misty's ears. Then, to Elizabeth's surprise, their mother let out a chuckle!

"Now I know where all the milk and tuna fish went to," Mrs. Wakefield said.

Elizabeth looked quickly at her sister. Their mother didn't sound angry at all!

"Aren't you angry at us?" Jessica asked timidly.

Their mother smiled. "No, I'm not angry. But you know you were wrong to hide Misty, don't you? Especially since Dad and Steven are allergic to cats."

Elizabeth and Jessica both nodded several times. Misty stood up and fussed with her blanket again. She let out a low meow before lying down. Then she started licking her stomach.

"But, Mom?" Elizabeth said. "What's wrong with her? We think she's sick. Look— her stomach hurts her."

"Let me see, now." Mrs. Wakefield petted

Misty's back, and felt her stomach very gently. She looked at the cat for a long time, and then smiled at the twins. "Misty's not sick," she announced.

Elizabeth's eyes lit up. "She's not?"

"But what's wrong with her?" Jessica asked.

Mrs. Wakefield petted Misty again. "I think she's going to have kittens."

Elizabeth's mouth dropped open. She stared at Jessica in surprise. "Kittens!" they both said at once.

"And very soon, too," their mother added. "From the way she's acting, I think it will be tonight."

Elizabeth gulped as she looked at Misty. "Can we watch?" she whispered.

"We can try," Mrs. Wakefield said. She took Elizabeth's hand, and reached for

Jessica's, too. "We don't want to frighten Misty. She may want to be alone. We'll have to be very quiet."

"We will," Jessica said solemnly.

"Hey, Mom?" Steven called. "Where—" He walked into the twins' room, and saw them all kneeling in front of the closet. "What's going on?"

"Come here, Steven!" Elizabeth said. "Look!"

Steven came over, and looked in at Misty. "Hey—"

"She's going to have babies!" Jessica said excitedly.

"Really? Cool!" Steven knelt down next to Elizabeth, and let out a sneeze. "Right here?"

"Right here," Mrs. Wakefield said. She looked excited, too. "We just have to wait until she's ready."

CHAPTER 10

Misty's New Family

Instead of eating dinner in the dining room that night, the Wakefields ate a picnic in the twins' bedroom. They wanted to be close to Misty in case she needed them. But they kept the lights low and the closet door nearly shut to give Misty privacy.

Mr. Wakefield opened a window for fresh air. "That should help a little bit," he said. He sneezed again and blew his nose.

"You don't mind, do you, Dad?" Jessica asked him. They had told him all about Misty when he had come home from work.

"Well . . ." He smiled at their mother. "We'll have to move Misty to the garage after the kittens are born," he said.

Jessica let out a sigh of relief. "That's OK."

Elizabeth tiptoed to the closet and peeked inside. "Hey, everyone!" Elizabeth whispered excitedly. "Come quick!"

Jessica dropped her sandwich on the plate and ran across the room. "What?" she whispered as she looked over Elizabeth's shoulder. Misty had her eyes closed, and she was panting even harder.

"I think it's time," Mrs. Wakefield said, also peeking in at the cat.

Everyone became so quiet that Jessica could hear her heart beating inside her. She held her breath.

"Meow!" cried Misty. She licked under her tail and then closed her eyes again.

"Oh," whispered Elizabeth. "Here comes a kitten!"

One by one, five tiny kittens came out, wet and sticky. Misty washed each one all over with her rough tongue. Her happy purr filled the big closet. Everyone was very quiet.

"A white one, a black one, and three like Misty," Jessica said softly, pointing to each one. She hugged her mother. "Aren't they cute?"

"They sure are," Mrs. Wakefield agreed.

"We're so lucky we found her," Elizabeth said.

Jessica laughed with happiness. "And *she's* lucky we found her, too."

Misty looked up, purring peacefully. The five little kittens snuggled close to her side. "Meow!" Misty said.

Jessica and Elizabeth looked at each other and smiled. They knew Misty agreed with them one hundred percent!

Jessica and Elizabeth ran all the way to the bus stop the next morning. They couldn't wait to find out if Caroline could keep Misty, and to tell her the big surprise, too!

"Caroline!" Jessica yelled when they saw her.

Caroline turned around. "Oh! Hey, guess what?" she said when she saw the twins.

"You guess what!" Elizabeth said.

"No, you guess what first," Caroline giggled.

Jessica hugged her books. "Do you get to have Misty?"

Caroline nodded. "Yes. My mother said I could."

"Great! Now *you* guess what," Jessica said. She looked at Elizabeth and laughed.

"I can't! Tell me!" Caroline said. "Is it good?"

"Yes, it's wonderful," Elizabeth said. "Misty had five kittens last night!"

"She did?" Caroline looked astonished. "I don't think I can have Misty and five kittens, too."

Jessica shook her head. "Our mother says we can find good homes for all of them."

"Phew," Caroline said with a smile. "I'm so excited about taking Misty home."

"You'll have to wait until the babies are big enough," Elizabeth told her.

Caroline nodded. "That's OK. I can wait."

As soon as Jessica and Elizabeth got to

school they made an announcement. "Misty had five kittens last night!" Jessica told everyone. "And we watched."

Eva raised her hand. "Oh! Can I have one of them? My mother said I could have another cat after we moved here."

"Me, too!" Winston pleaded. "Can I have one?"

"Not until the kittens are six weeks old," Elizabeth said. "They're living in our garage until then."

Lois tapped Jessica's elbow. "Could I have one? My mother says we always have room for another cat."

Jessica looked at her sister happily. Three of the five little kittens had just found good homes. And now that Misty would be living with Caroline, they could visit as often as they wanted. This was the next best thing to having a cat of their own.

After school, Jessica and Elizabeth visited Misty and the kittens in the garage. Now Misty had a water bowl, a dish of cat food, and a real litter box. She looked very happy.

"I hope she isn't afraid of sleeping out here," Jessica said.

Elizabeth smiled. "I'll bet she isn't. Cats aren't afraid of the dark."

"I would be!" Jessica said with a shiver. "Wouldn't it be scary to sleep outside?"

"No, it would be fun," Elizabeth said. She got an excited look in her eyes. "Why don't we try it sometime?" she suggested.

Jessica stared at her sister. "Are you crazy?"

Elizabeth laughed. "No, I think we should have a camp out."

"I don't know," Jessica said. "Just thinking about it gives me the creeps!"

Will the twins be brave enough to camp out all night? Find out in Sweet Valley Kids #6, LILA'S SECRET.